Plane's Royal Rescue

Peter Bently

Illustrated by Bella Bee and Lucy Fleming

Plane is at the airport preparing for a flight.

Captain Koala and his copilot watch as a fuel truck fills up the fuel tanks.

Luggage is loaded from a luggage cart into the **hold**.

A **pushback tug** is attached to Plane's **front wheels**.

A black **limousine** drives up
to a **private jet** nearby.

"It's the **king** and his family,"
says Captain Koala to his copilot.
"They're **flying** to the **same airport** as us."

A **bus** brings the **passengers** to Plane.

While they are **boarding**, the pilots
check everything in the **cockpit**.

There are lots of **dials** and
switches and computer screens.

The **royal jet** is now leaving. The limousine driver waves frantically at the **king's pilot**. But the pilot does not see him.

Captain Koala goes to **find out** what the matter is.

"The king's forgotten his **crown!**"
says the driver.

"**Don't worry**," smiles
Captain Koala. "I have an idea."

Plane's doors **close**. The boarding stairs are rolled away. It's time to go!

Captain Koala starts the **huge jets**. They **whirr** into life. The pilots check their computers to make sure everything is working.

The **tug** pushes Plane back from the **terminal**. Then the tug drives clear.

The copilot **powers** up the engines.

Plane moves toward the **runway**.

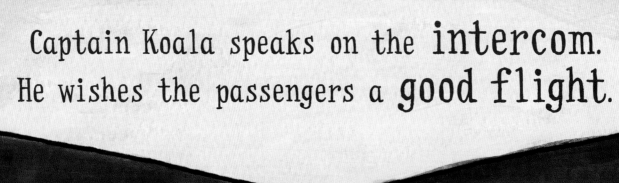

Captain Koala speaks on the **intercom**.
He wishes the passengers a **good flight**.

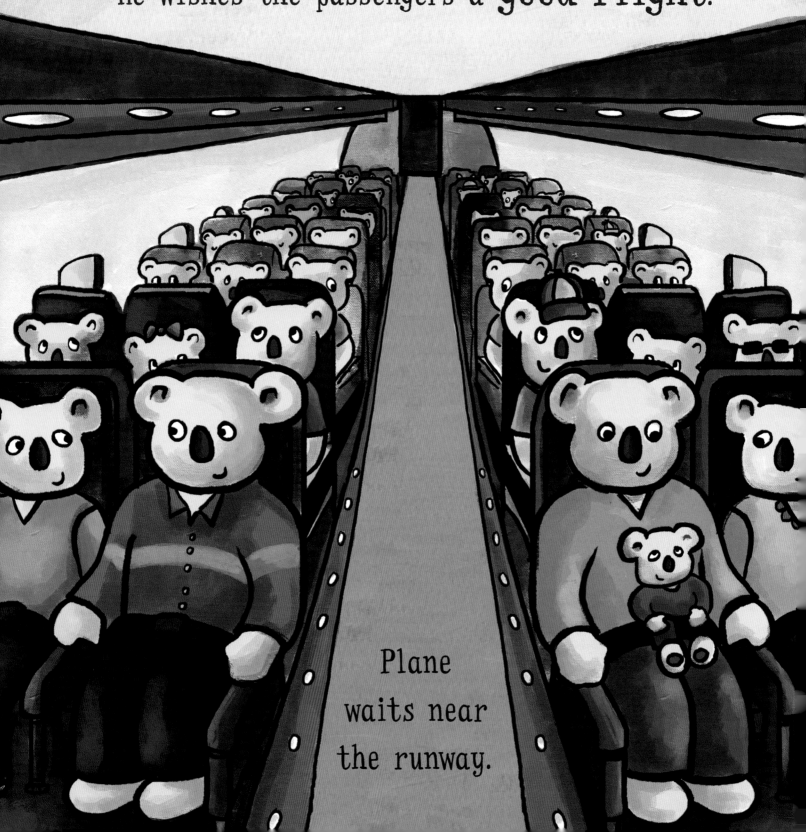

Plane
waits near
the runway.

A huge cargo jet takes off.

"You are clear for takeoff!"
says the air traffic controller.

Plane moves to the **start** of the **runway**.

WHOOSH!

Captain Koala puts the engines on **full power**.

Plane **speeds** down the runway and **takes off.**

ROAR!

THUNK!

Plane **tucks** in its wheels.

Plane **climbs** above the **clouds**
and into the sunshine.

The flight is **very smooth**.
Plane flies over **mountains** and **seas**.

At last Plane **descends** toward its
destination. The wheels **come down.**

CLUNK!

As they land, Captain Koala puts the engines into **reverse** to slow down.

ROAR!

Plane **taxies** to the terminal.

The **boarding steps** are moved into place.
Buses are waiting for the passengers.

As they leave, their luggage is
unloaded onto a **luggage cart.**

The royal jet is already
at the **terminal.**

"But **where** is my crown?"
asks a very **worried** king.
"I have an **important** event today!"

"Your Majesty, here is your crown,"
says Captain Koala. "We looked after
it **very** carefully in the cockpit!"

"Thank you, Captain Koala!" says the king.

"And thanks to Plane!" says Captain Koala.

Let's look at
Plane

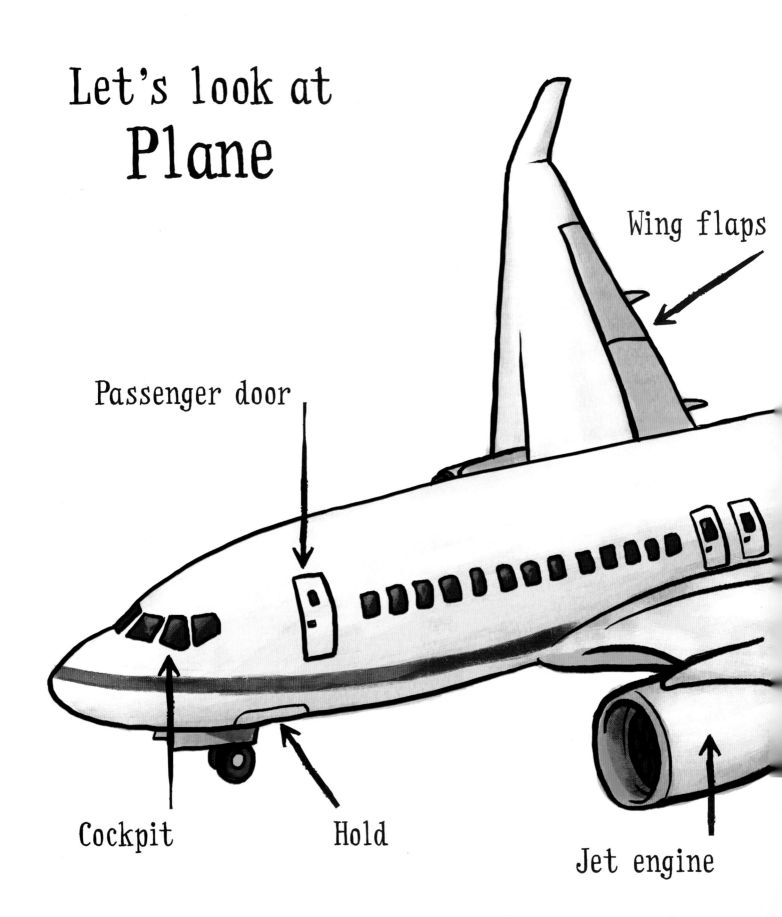

Wing flaps

Passenger door

Cockpit

Hold

Jet engine

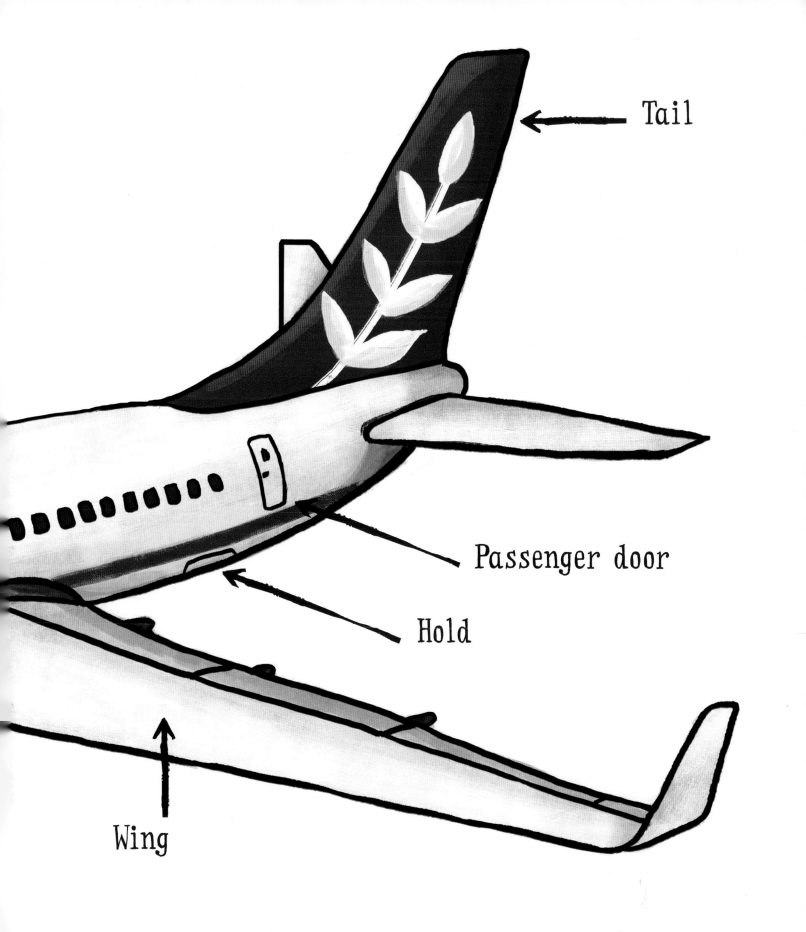

Tail

Passenger door

Hold

Wing

Other Airport Vehicles

Turboprop airliner

Pushback tug

Luggage cart

Helicopter

For my family P.B.

Designer: Rachel Lawston
Art Director: Laura Roberts-Jensen
Editors: Tasha Percy and Sophie Hallam
Editorial Director: Victoria Garrard

Copyright © QEB Publishing, Inc. 2015

First published in the United States by
QEB Publishing, Inc.
6 Orchard
Lake Forest, CA 92630

www.qed-publishing.co.uk

A CIP record for this book is available from the Library of Congress.

ISBN 978 1 60992 791 2

Printed in China